Editor: Rajani Thindiath

© Amar Chitra Katha Pvt Ltd, 2012, Reprinted December 2013, ISBN 978-81-8482-700-2
Published & Printed by Amar Chitra Katha Pvt. Ltd., Krishna House, 3rd Floor,
Raghuvanshi Mill Compound, S.B.Marg, Lower Parel (W), Mumbai- 400 013. India
For Consumer Complaints Contact Tel : +91-22 40497436
Email: customerservice@ack-media.com

Dear readers,

Here's presenting a collection of the childhood adventures of *Tinkle*'s most darling hunter, Shikari Shambu.

*The Adventures of Little Shambu* was the brainwave of Reena I. Puri, then the Associate Editor of *Tinkle* and now Editor, *Amar Chitra Katha*.

For me, it was a challenge to draw the junior version of the character. And as you all know, no one has ever seen Shikari Shambu's eyes. We did have a discussion, to figure out if we wanted to show Little Shambu's eyes, but decided against it as it would take away from the character. I tried all sort of hats to cover his eyes and finally settled on the beige-coloured cotton hat you now see. I kept his looks the same, short and stout, with his belly button showing.

The editorial team always felt that Shanti was portrayed unnecessarily as a nag all the time. With Little Shambu we got a chance to give her a happier character— the girl who moves into the neighbourhood along with her cat, Kittu. Drawing Shanti was fun. I based her on my colleague's little daughter.

Even J. J. appears as the nasty kid who is always trying to get Little Shambu into trouble. I hope you know that J. J. is short for Jeeva Jeevantak!

And finally we had to give him a friend and Reena, being an animal lover, came up with a dog named, Dum Dum.

Little Shambu first appeared in *Tinkle* 434, January 2000.

Reena and I had a wonderful journey with Little Shambu. Hope you enjoy reading the stories as much as we did writing and illustrating them.

– *Savio A. Mascarenhas*

## CAT CALL

By: Reena I. Puri

Illustrations:
Savio Mascarenhas

3

LITTLE SHAMBU TRUDGED DOWN NEVER-ENDING ROADS...

...HE LOOKED THROUGH JUNGLE-LIKE BACKYARDS...

...AND FORDED MANY RIVERS AND LAKES...

...TILL HE REACHED A HIGH MOUNTAIN RANGE.

I MUST SCALE THE PEAK. MAYBE THE MAN-EATER IS ON THE OTHER SIDE.

UNGH...OOF... I'M THERE...

...OH...OH... I AM LOSING MY...

...BALANCE!

5

# THE ADVENTURES OF LITTLE SHAMBU

## THE CARROT THIEF

By: Reena I. Puri

Illustrations:
Savio Mascarenhas

LITTLE SHAMBU WAS GETTING A SCOLDING.

IF YOU CAN'T KEEP THAT DOG OF YOURS IN CONTROL HE MUST GO. HE HAS DUG UP ALL THE CARROTS.

GRRR

LATER —

WHY DO YOU HAVE TO DIG UP THE CARROT PATCH, DUM DUM?

WOOF WOOF

YOU'VE MADE SUCH HUGE HOLES IN IT.

HAS YOUR DUM DUM DONE THAT?

IT WAS LITTLE SHAMBU'S NEW NEIGHBOUR, SHANTI, WITH HER CAT, KITTU.

WHAT A SILLY DOG!

MY KITTU WOULD NEVER DO ANYTHING SO...

MEOWRR

GRROWL

YAAAH!

HA! HA! HA! YOUR KITTU HAS MADE YOU LOOK LIKE AN ELECTRIFIED POLE.

MAMA!

NOW I'LL GET INTO TROUBLE WITH HER PARENTS AS WELL. I HAD BETTER BECOME INVISIBLE FOR A WHILE.

LITTLE SHAMBU CROUCHED BEHIND SOME BUSHES AND FELL ASLEEP. AND THEN HE HAD A DREAM.

I'M LATE! I'M LATE, FOR AN IMPORTANT DATE.

IT'S DUM DUM, AND HE'S GOING DOWN THAT HOLE. I MUST FOLLOW HIM...

...BUT WHY IS HE DRESSED LIKE A RABBIT?

# THE ADVENTURES OF LITTLE SHAMBU

## NIBBLE NIBBLE

By: Reena I. Puri

Illustrations:
Savio Mascarenhas

THERE WAS CONFUSION IN THE SHAMBU HOUSEHOLD.

BLAST! OUTRAGEOUS! DASH IT!

I THINK YOUR FATHER IS UPSET.

DUM DUM

SUHASINI, LOOK AT MY SOCKS.

OH DEAR, WHAT ENORMOUS HOLES!

A RAT GOT YOUR SOCKS, PA.

I KNOW THAT, SHERLOCK HOLMES! SET A RAT TRAP TONIGHT.

LATER —

GET THE RAT TRAP FROM THE LOFT, SON.

I'LL SET IT UP TONIGHT, MA.

THAT NIGHT —

I'LL KEEP THE RAT TRAP NEAR THE DOOR. THE PIECE OF CHEESE SHOULD BRING THE RAT STRAIGHT HERE.

THAT NIGHT THE MOON ROSE AS USUAL INTO THE SKY. ALL WAS PEACEFUL AND QUIET, TILL...

...A PIERCING SHRIEK RENT THE AIR.

AAIEEEOOO

DASH! BLAST! GET IT OFF!

OH NO!

PA'S WALKED INTO THE RAT TRAP.

YOU SHOULD LOOK WHERE YOU ARE GOING.

SHALL I SET THE TRAP AGAIN?

NO!

THE NEXT MORNING—

SUHASINI! LOOK AT THESE HOLES IN MY VEST. THAT WRETCHED RAT HAS BEEN AT IT AGAIN.

WHY DOES IT PICK ON YOU, PA?

DON'T GET SMART WITH ME. I'LL CALL THE RAT EXTERMINATOR TO FINISH OFF THAT RODENT.

GOSH! THAT SOUNDS TOUGH.

THE RAT EXTERMINATOR WAS A VERY EFFICIENT MAN.

I'VE PUT RAT POISON IN EVERY NOOK AND CRANNY AND SET TRAPS OF EVERY SIZE AND SHAPE...

HEY RAT, STAND HERE ↓

FOR RATS ONLY

SAY CHEESE!

...YOU WON'T HAVE A PROBLEM NOW.

GOOD!

THIS PLACE LOOKS LIKE A TORTURE CHAMBER.

RATS WILL BE PERSESUTED HA! HA! HA!

SEE THAT THE DOG DOESN'T EAT THE POISON OR IT WILL BE A DEAD DOG. HA! HA! HA!

FUNNY, EH!

GROWL

LATER—

I FEEL QUITE SORRY FOR THE RAT. IMAGINE BEING HUNTED LIKE THIS...

...IMAGINE BEING HATED SO MUCH...

...DOESN'T A RAT NEED FOOD?

...DON'T YOU THINK IT WOULD FEEL HUNGRY?

JUST THEN —

EEEEK!

WH...WHAT?

SQUEAK

WOOF!

A M...M...MOUSE IN YOUR B...B...BLOUSE... I MEAN... SHIRT.

IT'S THE LITTLE FELLOW!

YOU ARE NOT EVEN A RAT. YOU ARE A LITTLE MOUSE...

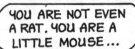

MEOW!

...AND HERE COMES THAT TERMINATOR GUY.

LET'S GET AWAY BEFORE HE SEES YOU.

DEEP IN THE FOREST—

RUN OFF, LITTLE MOUSE, AND DON'T COME NEAR MY HOUSE AGAIN.

SQUEAK!

BACK AT HOME —

....YOU SHOULD HAVE SEEN HOW BRAVE YOUR SON WAS. HE CAUGHT THIS HUGE, MONSTROUS RAT BY THE TAIL AND TOOK IT AWAY.

THAT'S MY BRAVE BOY! JUST LIKE HIS FATHER.

# THE ADVENTURES OF LITTLE SHAMBU

## IN THE BEAR'S LAIR

By: Reena I. Puri

Illustrations:
Savio Mascarenhas

THERE WAS MUCH EXCITEMENT IN THE SHAMBU HOUSEHOLD.

YIPPEE! WE ARE GOING TO THE **ZOO**!

IS THERE ANY WAY WE CAN LEAVE HIM THERE?

SHH...DON'T BE MEAN!

LITTLE SHANTI JOINED THEM FOR THE TRIP.

I'VE BEEN HERE BEFORE, SO I CAN SHOW YOU EVERYTHING.

NATIO ZOO

NOT FAR AWAY —

WHAT'S THAT SHINY THING THERE?

IT WAS KAMMO, THE CURIOUS TIGER CUB.

MAMA IS SLEEPING. I CAN SNEAK AWAY AND HAVE A LOOK.

THE SHINY THING WAS A BALL.

HEE! HEE! THIS IS FUN.

WATCH OUT KAMMO, YOU ARE HEADING FOR THE...

...OH NO!

YIPES!

15

SHAMBU AND DUM DUM TRIED TO GET AS HIGH UP ON THE ROCKS AS POSSIBLE.

I DON'T WANT TO BE BEAR DINNER. I CANNOT OVERFEED THE BEAR WITH MYSELF.

SNARL

GROWL

JUST THEN —

URRR!?

PING!

THE BEAR KEEPER HAD SHOT A TRANQUILLISER* DART AT THE BEAR.

ARE YOU ALL RIGHT, LITTLE BOY?

HE WENT IN TO SAVE HIS DOG...

WOOF WOOF

...AND LOOK, HE HAS EVEN FOUND THE LOST TIGER CUB.

I HAVE?

WOOF! PURR!

YES, IT WAS KAMMO, THE TIGER CUB, WHO HAD EARLIER FALLEN INTO THE BEAR PIT.

WE WERE LOOKING FOR HER ALL OVER. THE BEAR WOULD HAVE GOT HER.

JUST THEN —

I AM SORRY! MY SON HAS BEEN A NUISANCE. I WILL...

ON THE CONTRARY, SIR, HE IS A BRAVE LAD. WE ARE GIVING HIM ONE YEAR'S FREE ENTRY TO THE ZOO.

* A DRUG THAT CAN MAKE A PERSON OR ANIMAL, CALM OR UNCONSCIOUS.

18

# THE ADVENTURES OF LITTLE SHAMBU

## THE CASE OF STRANGUS DERANGUS

By: Reena I. Puri

Illustrations:
Savio Mascarenhas

IT WAS A LAZY AFTERNOON—

I AM GETTING BORED. LET'S DO SOMETHING EXCITING.

LIKE WHAT?

LIKE... UM... EARN SOME MONEY TO BUY ICE CREAM.

GOOD IDEA! BUT HOW DO WE DO THAT?

MUMMY'S FRIEND EARNED MONEY BY HOLDING AN EXHIBITION OF CLOTHES.

WHO WOULD WANT TO SEE OUR CLOTHES?

STOP ASKING QUESTIONS!

WHY?

...OKAY! OKAY!

I THINK I KNOW WHAT WE CAN EXHIBIT.

TELL ME!

THERE ARE LOTS OF THINGS WE CAN EXHIBIT. COME ON, I'LL SHOW YOU. THEY ARE ALL HERE IN THE GARDEN AND BEHIND THE KITCHEN.

IN THE MEANWHILE —

AS SOON AS THE GUESTS COME, YOU MUST SERVE HOT TEA AND SAMOSAS. THIS MEETING HAS TO BE PERFECT, MY PROMOTION DEPENDS ON IT.

STOP WORRYING!

SHAMBU, WHAT DO YOU HAVE IN THAT BAG?

SHAMBU, WHAT ARE YOU DOING HERE?

NOTHING, MA. I AM NOT HERE, PA.

EH?

GOSH! I THOUGHT PA WOULD ASK US TO OPEN THE BAG.

ARE YOU SURE YOUR FRIENDS WILL WANT TO SEE ALL THESE COCKROACHES AND MICE?

OF COURSE!

YECH! THEY LOOK QUITE CREEPY.

20

I THINK WE SHOULD HAVE A STAR ATTRACTION.

LIKE WHAT?

LIKE... LIKE AN UNUSUAL BEAST.

HMM...I GET WHAT YOU MEAN.

OH NO! WHY ARE THEY LOOKING AT ME?

BEFORE LONG —

DUM DUM IS THE STRANGE BEAST FROM A FAR OFF LAND.

YES, WE'LL CALL HIM STRANGUS DERANGUS — ALL ANIMALS MUST HAVE LATIN NAMES.

THE NEWS GOT AROUND THAT THERE WAS AN EXHIBITION OF UNKNOWN ANIMALS AT LITTLE SHAMBU'S HOUSE.

IT COSTS 50 PAISE PER HEAD. DROP YOUR COINS IN HERE.

AND DON'T MAKE A NOISE OR THE STRANGUS DERANGUS MIGHT ATTACK.

BEWARE OF THE STRANGUS DERANGUS

THIS IS EXHIBIT 'A' — THE MARTIAN DUST CRAWLER.

RUBBISH! IT'S A COCKROACH.

YOU HAVE NO IMAGINATION.

AND THIS HOPPER BOPPER IS ONLY A MOUSE.

HOPPER BO

WHAT ABOUT STRANGUS DERANGUS? IT IS REAL.

WELL... ER... I...

IT'S DUM DUM!

CATCH HIM!

WOOF! WOOF!!

WE'VE BEEN CHEATED!

THE ANGRY CHILDREN CHASED LITTLE SHAMBU RIGHT THROUGH THE HOUSE.

YAAARGH!

SHAMBU!

HEY!

WHAT'S HAPPENING?

WHEN THE DUST HAD SETTLED—

I BEG YOUR PARDON, SIR... MY SON... HE...

SPEAK NO MORE...

...YOUR SON IS A GENIUS. WHAT A BRILLIANT MARKETING IDEA! NEW PACKAGING FOR OLD ITEMS. HIS FATHER MUST BE CLEVERER...

...CONGRATULATIONS! YOU ARE OUR NEXT CHIEF MANAGER.

HEH! HEH! MY SON!

22

# THE ADVENTURES OF LITTLE SHAMBU

## NO TIFFIN FOR J.J.

By: Reena I. Puri

Illustrations: Savio Mascarenhas

LITTLE SHAMBU WAS GETTING READY FOR SCHOOL.

HERE'S YOUR TIFFIN, SON.

NO POINT.

WHAT DO YOU MEAN BY NO POINT?

I MEAN THAT I WON'T GET TO EAT IT...

...J.J. WILL. HE ALWAYS TAKES MY TIFFIN.

WELL, LEARN TO PROTECT YOUR TIFFIN. I AM KEEPING IT HERE.

MUMMY DOESN'T KNOW WHAT A HORRID BULLY J.J. IS.

J.J. WAS JEEVA JEEVANTAK, THE SCHOOL BULLY.

AS SHAMBU WALKED TO SCHOOL—

LOOK WHO'S HERE! A HARMLESS LITTLE GARDEN SNAKE!

POOR THING! IT LOOKS WEAK AND ILL. IT'S THOSE SNAKE CATCHERS. THEY CATCH SNAKES FOR THE SNAKE FESTIVAL AND THEN ABANDON THEM. MEAN FELLOWS!

I'LL KEEP IT IN MY SCHOOL BAG AND LEAVE IT IN THE FIELDS AFTER SCHOOL.

SHAMBU WAS A LITTLE LATE REACHING SCHOOL THAT DAY.

HALT! LATE AGAIN, YOUNG SHAMBU! WHAT IS YOUR EXCUSE THIS TIME?

A SNAKE. I SAW A POOR SNAKE AND...

STORIES! STORIES! WHAT A WILD IMAGINATION YOU HAVE! GO AND SIT IN YOUR PLACE.

STUPID SHAMBU... GETS A FIRING EVERY DAY.

KEEP QUIET, J.J.

MEANWHILE THE LITTLE SNAKE WHICH HAD COLLAPSED DUE TO THE HEAT ON THE CONCRETE PAVEMENT...

...REVIVED IN THE COOL OF SHAMBU'S SCHOOL BAG.

I LIKE IT IN HERE.

THE WATCHMAN CAME BRANDISHING A LARGE STICK.

KILL THAT SNAKE. KILL IT AT ONCE.

WHY DO YOU WANT TO KILL IT?

BUT THE WATCHMAN WOULD NOT LISTEN.

DON'T KILL IT! STOP IT! IT'S HARMLESS!

THWACK THWACK

!

LUCKILY FOR THE LITTLE SNAKE THE OLD GARDENER OF THE SCHOOL CAME IN.

MANU KAKA, TELL THEM THAT THIS IS A HARMLESS SNAKE. THEY ARE KILLING IT.

OF COURSE IT IS HARMLESS...

...IN FACT THIS LITTLE FELLOW IS A FRIEND.

A FRIEND?

YES. THIS GARDEN SNAKE EATS RATS AND OTHER PESTS THAT DESTROY PLANTS. I'LL TAKE HIM. I KNOW THE PLACE FOR HIM.

THAT DAY AFTER SCHOOL SHAMBU WENT WITH MANU KAKA TO THE FIELDS OUTSIDE TOWN.

THERE YOU ARE, LITTLE ONE. GO HOME.

HE LOOKS HAPPY, DOESN'T HE?

CALL ME IF THAT BULLY TAKES YOUR TIFFIN AGAIN.

# Little Shambu

By: Savio

# THE ADVENTURES OF LITTLE SHAMBU

## PANDA PERILS

Story: Reena I. Puri

Script: Gayathri Chandrasekaran

Illustrations: Savio Mascarenhas

LITTLE SHAMBU AND HIS PARENTS WERE GOING TO THE AIRPORT TO RECEIVE HIS AUNT.

HURRY UP, LITTLE SHAMBU, THE PLANE WILL BE LANDING SOON.

COMING, MA.

LITTLE SHAMBU'S AUNT WAS ARRIVING FROM CHINA.

I HOPE SHE HAS REMEMBERED TO BUY ME DRAGON SHOES.

I HOPE SO TOO BUT WHAT ARE YOU HIDING BEHIND YOUR BACK?

SORRY, DUM DUM CANNOT COME ALONG.

AW, PA! I CAN'T LEAVE HIM ALONE AT HOME!

OF COURSE YOU CAN. NOW STOP FUSSING AND GO WEAR YOUR SHOES.

A FEW SECONDS LATER—

LET'S GO!

SOON—

SSSSH! SOME AIR FOR YOU, DUM DUM.

29

31

# THE ADVENTURES OF LITTLE SHAMBU

**Rattle on the Cattle**

Story: Aditi Jayakar

Script: Reena I. Puri

Illustrations: Savio Mascarenhas

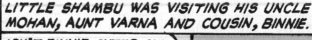

LITTLE SHAMBU WAS VISITING HIS UNCLE MOHAN, AUNT VARNA AND COUSIN, BINNIE.

ISN'T BINNIE CUTE? SHE LOVES HER COUSIN.

GURGLE... GOO... GOO!

YAAAAAA!

LITTLE SHAMBU WAS NOT SO FOND OF BINNIE BUT HE ENJOYED UNCLE MOHAN'S FARM.

HOW DO YOU DO?

MOO MOO

HE TRIED TO SWIM WITH THE DUCKS, BUT—

OKAY... OKAY... I WON'T COME IF YOU DON'T WANT TO SHARE YOUR POND.

QUACK! QUACK!

ONE DAY—

LITTLE SHAMBU, THERE'S A LOT OF FRESH, GREEN GRASS ON THAT HILL. WILL YOU GRAZE THE COWS FOR ME THERE?

ALL RIGHT, UNCLE MOHAN.

ANYTHING TO GET AWAY FROM BINNIE.

SO, THE NEXT MORNING—

THEY LOOK SO HUGE. I HOPE THEY LISTEN TO ME.

LITTLE SHAMBU SPENT THE DAY SKETCHING THE BEAUTIFUL HILLS AND FIELDS...

...BUT WHEN IT WAS TIME TO HEAD BACK—

I CAN SEE ONLY TWO COWS. WHERE ARE THE OTHER THREE ?

HE FOUND THEM AFTER A LONG SEARCH...

THERE THEY ARE! GET HERE, ALL OF YOU!

...AND HEADED BACK HOME.

IT'S SO DARK. AUNT VARNA MUST BE WORRIED.

AND SO SHE WAS.

THANK HEAVENS YOU ARE HERE. THERE ARE WOLVES IN THE FOREST. IT CAN BE DANGEROUS AFTER SUNSET.

WHILE HE WAS EATING HIS DINNER, LITTLE SHAMBU HAD AN IDEA.

I'LL TAKE BINNIE'S RATTLES AND TIE THEM TO THE COWS. THEN I'LL KNOW EXACTLY WHERE THEY ARE.

SO, AFTER DINNER—

THESE RATTLES AND BELLS SHOULD DO. I'LL TIE THEM TO THE HORNS OF THE COWS.

OFF HE WENT TO THE COWSHED.

SORRY, MRS. MOO, I NEED TO DECORATE YOU AND YOUR FAMILY.

BEFORE LONG —

THERE YOU ARE! HA! HA! YOU DO LOOK FUNNY!

RATTLE

RATTLE

TING TING

THEN HE WENT TO SPEND SOME TIME WITH HIS AUNT AND UNCLE.

OH, HERE YOU ARE! WHERE HAVE YOU BEEN?

ER.. I WAS IN BINNIE'S ROOM.

SAYING GOODNIGHT, EH?

BINNIE IS VERY FOND OF YOU. I MUST SEND HER TO SPEND TIME WITH YOU WHEN SHE GROWS UP.

OH DEAR!

YOU MUST HAVE LEFT HER IN A CHEERFUL MOOD. I CAN HEAR HER PLAYING WITH HER RATTLE.

YEH...HEH... HEH...WELL...

...RATTLE!?

LITTLE SHAMBU DASHED OUT...

35

# THE ADVENTURES OF LITTLE SHAMBU

**SERVES J.J. RIGHT!**

Readers' Choice

Based on a story sent by:
Tejas Mhetras, Parvati, Pune.

Illustrations: Savio Mascarenhas

LITTLE SHAMBU'S COUSIN HAD SENT HIM A COMIC BOOK ON DINOSAURS FROM THE U.S.

IT'S GOT A CASSETTE OF DINOSAUR SOUNDS AS WELL.

LITTLE SHAMBU PLAYED THE CASSETTE.

ROAR ROAR ROAR

BRR... THEY SOUND SCARY.

SUDDENLY—

YEOWL

THAT'S NOT FROM THE CASSETTE.

HE RAN OUTSIDE.

DID YOU YEOWL?

NO. IT WAS MY KITTU.

THAT HORRID J.J. THREW A STONE AT HER.

THAT'S MEAN OF YOU, J.J.

37

THE BIG TOMCAT AND J.J. JUMPED OUT OF THEIR SKINS.

YOWWRR!

YOW!

THUD!

MIAOW!

SCREECH

SCRATCH

RRRIP

OOH! OUCH!

SERVES HIM RIGHT.

OOH! SHAMBU! HOW CLEVER OF YOU TO SWITCH ON THAT TAPE.

IT WAS NOTHING.

OH, HOW BRAVE OF YOU TO FIGHT J.J.!

MEOWRR.

# THE ADVENTURES OF LITTLE SHAMBU

**SHOOTING WITH A BEAR**

Story Idea : S. Charulata

Script : Reena I. Puri

Illustrations: Savio Mascarenhas

LITTLE SHAMBU WAS VERY EXCITED.

WILL WE SEE REAL FILM ACTORS?

OF COURSE. MASTER BULLOO WILL BE THERE. HE IS MY FAVOURITE.

HE WAS GOING WITH SHANTI, HIS NEIGHBOUR, TO SEE A FILM BEING SHOT.

SILLY NAME, BUL-L-L-O-O-O!

BETTER THAN SHAM-B-O-O-O-O.

SOON—

THERE IS THE FILM UNIT. WATCH FROM A DISTANCE AND DON'T GET IN THE WAY.

YES, DADDY.

EXCUSE ME. WHERE IS MASTER BULLOO?

HE IS CHANGING INTO A BEAR CUB COSTUME. HE WEARS IT IN THE FILM TO SCARE HIS TEACHER AT A CAMP.

HOW SWEET!

HOW SILLY!

NOT FAR AWAY—

STOP SULKING! IF YOU DON'T DANCE, WE GET NOTHING TO EAT.

GLOOM.

MUNNI, THE DANCING BEAR, WAS VERY SAD...

...BECAUSE HER BABY WAS LOST.

YOUR BABY CAN'T BE FAR. WE'LL FIND HIM.

SOB!

MEANWHILE—

THAT IS MY FRIEND, SHANTI. COME AND TALK TO HER NICELY. I'LL SHARE A SANDWICH WITH YOU IF YOU DO THAT.

HEY, SHANTI, LOOK WHO I BROUGHT TO MEET YOU. THIS IS MASTER BULLOO IN HIS BEAR COSTUME.

OOOH! MASTER BULLOO.

I'VE SEEN EVERY FILM OF YOURS.

I LIKE YOU SO MUCH.

NICE HUMAN.

OH! HOW SWEET!

42

43

# THE ADVENTURES OF LITTLE SHAMBU
## FINDING LAKSHMI

Story & Script:
Reena I. Puri

Illustrations:
Savio Mascarenhas

LITTLE SHAMBU WAS ON A HOLIDAY WITH HIS PARENTS.

KERALA IS SO BEAUTIFUL.

IT IS SO HOT AND STICKY.

CAN I HAVE A BATH LIKE THEM?

NO!

SOME CHILDREN HERE EVEN GO TO SCHOOL BY BOAT.

THEY ARE HAVING SO MUCH FUN.

CAN I HAVE A BOAT WITH WHEELS TO GO TO SCHOOL IN?

NO!

NOT FAR AWAY —

I AM TIRED OF STANDING HERE AND EATING BANANAS.

IT WAS LAKSHMI, THE TEMPLE BABY ELEPHANT.

I THINK I'LL GO FOR A WALK.

BEFORE LONG —

WHERE IS LAKSHMI? I JUST LEFT HER HERE.

OH NO! LAKSHMI IS LOST. SHE HAS BEEN ELEPHANT-NAPPED.

MEANWHILE — LOOK, SHAMBU, THERE IS THAT BOY FROM YOUR CLASS.

SHEESH! WHAT BAD LUCK. IT'S J.J.

J.J. WAS THE CLASS BULLY.

ISN'T THIS ROLY-POLY SHAMBU? FORGOTTEN YOUR SHIRT, PUDDING?

LEAVE ME ALONE, J.J.

HELLO! HAVEN'T I SEEN YOU AT MY SON'S SCHOOL?

YES. I THINK OUR BOYS ARE IN THE SAME CLASS.

AND SO —

THE BOYS CAN KEEP EACH OTHER COMPANY WHILE WE VISIT THE TEMPLE.

YOU'LL LIKE THAT, WON'T YOU?

SOMETIMES GROWN-UPS HAVE NO IDEA OF THE TROUBLE THEY CAN CAUSE.

NO, I AM NOT. I AM GOING AWAY.

YOU'RE AT MY MERCY, SHAMBU.

COME BACK, SHAMBU.

AIEEEE!

NO, I WON'T.

IT'S NOT EASY RUNNING IN THESE CLOTHES. MAY BE I SHOULD TUCK IT UP LIKE THOSE MEN.

# THE ADVENTURES OF LITTLE SHAMBU

## THE SLUGGISH SNAKE

By: Prabha Nair

Illustrations: Savio Mascarenhas

LITTLE SHAMBU'S MOTHER WAS CLEANING UP THE HOUSE.

WHAT A MESS! SHOES HERE, BOOKS THERE...

SHE WENT INTO THE BATHROOM —

...AND GOODNESS ME, A TOWEL ON THE FLOOR.

WATER HOLE

SHE BENT DOWN TO PICK IT UP AND —

SCREECH!

LITTLE SHAMBU CAME RUNNING IN.

MAMA! WHY DID YOU SCREAM?

IT'S A SNAKE! A MONSTER!

WOW! LET ME SEE!

NO! NO! DON'T OPEN THAT DOOR. I'LL CALL KONDIAH TO GET RID OF IT.

KONDIAH, THE WATCHMAN? HE'LL KILL IT. HE HATES ANIMALS.

LITTLE SHAMBU CREPT INTO THE BATHROOM.

IT'S A GARDEN SNAKE. BUT WHAT A BEAUTY!

SHAMBU KNEW HE HAD NOTHING TO FEAR FROM A GARDEN SNAKE, SO HE OPENED THE DOOR WIDE.

HEY, SNAKE! GO AWAY QUICKLY.

(YAWN!)WHAT A NOISY HOUSEHOLD. WHY CAN'T THEY LET ME SLEEP IN PEACE?

HAVE TO PROD THIS LAZY SNAKE WITH SOMETHING TO MAKE IT MOVE.

SHAMBU GOT A CURTAIN ROD.

SHOO! SHOO!

OKAY! STOP POKING. I'LL GO.

SHAMBU POKED ITS TAIL AGAIN.

PLEASE GO! PLEASE!

MUST GET OUT OF THIS KID'S REACH.

IT SNAKED ITS WAY TO THE TOP OF THE CUPBOARD.

AAAH! NOW FOR MY SIESTA.

BUT LITTLE SHAMBU DID NOT GIVE UP.

HE DRAGGED IN A STOOL.

GO OUT OF THE VENTILATOR. HURRY! PLEASE.

ALL RIGHT. ALL RIGHT. I GET THE MESSAGE. I'M NOT WANTED HERE.

THE SNAKE SQUEEZED ITSELF BETWEEN THE VENTILATOR SLATS. BUT MIDWAY THROUGH—

WHOOPS! I'M STUCK! I'M FEELING SICK.

AND THE SNAKE THREW UP.

YECH!

UGH!

SHAMBU PEERED AT THE GLOP.

IT'S MOVING!

HE SAW THE GLOP HOP.

IT'S A FROG!

MY BREAKFAST!

SHAMBU RAN OUTDOORS.

THERE'S THE SNAKE ON THE BRANCH.

JUST THEN SHAMBU HEARD THE SOUND OF POUNDING FEET.

IT'S KONDIAH AND SOME OTHERS.

THE SNAKE! WHERE IS IT?

UH... IT WENT THAT WAY.

COME ON, MEN! LET'S KILL IT.

THAT NASTY MAN WITH THE STICK MUST HAVE COME TO KILL ME.

THANKS, KID. YOU SAVED MY LIFE.

I NEED A BATH.

# THE ADVENTURES OF LITTLE SHAMBU

## PROFESSOR Y. RUSS AND HIS MOUSE

Readers' Choice

Based on a story by:
A. S. Jagan Nadhan, Bengaluru

Illustrations: Savio Mascarenhas

LITTLE SHAMBU AND J. J., THE SCHOOL BULLY, WERE GOING TO THE BIOLOGY LABORATORY.

WHAT ARE YOU GOING TO BE DRESSED AS, FOR THE FANCY DRESS COMPETITION NEXT WEEK, SHAMBU?

MY FAVOURITE WRESTLER, THE ROCK.

'THE PEBBLE' WOULD BE A BETTER NAME FOR YOU, YOU LITTLE TWERP.

(GIGGLE)

SPURRED ON BY SHANTI'S GIGGLES —

HEY, PEBBLE, LET'S HAVE A WRESTLING MATCH.

MY NAME'S NOT 'PEBBLE'!

YOU CAN'T HAVE A WRESTLING MATCH IN SCHOOL. IT'S AGAINST THE RULES.

I MEANT AN ARM-WRESTLING MATCH.

OOH! SAY 'YES', SHAMBU.

WELL... WELL... OKAY.

A CHOCOLATE BAR FOR THE WINNER.

MEANWHILE IN THE BIOLOGY LAB, CHUHI, THE BIOLOGY TEACHER'S PET MOUSE, HAD MADE A HAPPY DISCOVERY.

FREEDOM!

CHUI

BUT DANGER LURKED BENEATH THE TABLE.

YOW! IT'S FLUFFY, THE SCHOOL CAT!

MEOWRRR

MEAOW!

SQUEAK!

THE CAT AND THE MOUSE STREAKED TOWARDS THE DOOR JUST AS...

...LITTLE SHAMBU AND THE OTHERS WALKED IN.

YAAAAH!

FLUFFY HEARD THE BLOOD-CURDLING YELL.

EEEEK!

SCRREECH

THAT WAS QUICK THINKING, SHAMBU. YOU FRIGHTENED HER AWAY WITH THAT YELL.

HSSSSST!

IT WAS PROFESSOR Y. RUSS, THE BIOLOGY TEACHER.

DID I?

BUT WHERE HAS CHUHI GONE... I'D BETTER FIND HER. I'LL BE BACK IN A JIFFY.

54

LITTLE SHAMBU ACTED FAST.

YAY! SHAMBU WINS!

THUMP!

AS J.J. HANDED OVER THE CHOCOLATE BAR—

IT'S NOT FAIR. I GOT SCARED BY THE MOUSE IN YOUR POCKET.

MOUSE!?

CALL ME NAMES, WILL YOU? BLE..AH!

LITTLE SHAMBU PUT HIS HAND IN HIS POCKET AND —

YIKES!

MEAOW!

HULLO, SHAMBU.

WHY, SHE'S SO CUTE!

FEED HER TO FLUFFY, SHAMBU.

I HEARD THAT, J.J. I DISLIKE CHILDREN WHO ENJOY HARMING MICE OR LIZARDS OR BUTTERFLIES OR...

ULP!...I... ER...I...AM SORRY, SIR.

LATER —

GRR....

THANKS FOR SAVING CHUHI, SHAMBU.

I DIDN'T, SIR. SHE SAVED HERSELF BY HIDING IN MY COAT POCKET.

AND HELPED YOU WIN THE MATCH TOO.

55

# MICE AT PLAY

## The Adventures of Little Shambu

Based on a story sent by: Aishwarya, Andheri, Mumbai

Illustrations: Savio Mascarenhas

LITTLE SHAMBU'S CLASS WAS VERY EXCITED. THEIR TEACHER MISS SHEILA WAS MAKING AN IMPORTANT ANNOUNCEMENT.

CHILDREN, FOR OUR ANNUAL DAY, WE WILL PERFORM 'CINDERELLA'. WHO WANTS TO TAKE PART?

ME! ME!

EVERYONE WAS ASKED TO RECITE A FEW LINES.

O FAIRY GODMOTHER, I WANT TO GO TO THE BALL! BUT ALAS, I HAVE NEITHER A DRESS NOR SHOES!

GOOD, LITTLE SHANTI, YOU WILL BE CINDERELLA. ALL THOSE WHO WANT TO BE THE PRINCE, COME FORWARD.

BOTH LITTLE SHAMBU AND J.J. WANTED TO BE THE PRINCE.

LET ME TRIP YOU, LITTLE SHAMBU. HEE HEE...

AND—

TUMBLE

SMASH

THUD

UNFORTUNATELY FOR LITTLE J.J.—

I SAW THAT, LITTLE JJ. HOW DARE YOU FOOL AROUND IN CLASS? GO TO THE END OF THE LINE.

ERR... ERR... SORRY, SHEILA MA'AM.

LITTLE SHAMBU GAVE A GOOD PERFORMANCE AND BECAME THE PRINCE!

IT WAS HARD WORK FOR LITTLE SHAMBU. HE PRACTISED HIS LINES...

MARRY ME, DUM DUM... ERR... I MEAN CINDERELLA.

WOOF WOOF!

...MADE A PUMPKIN...

SNIP

SNIP

GLUE

...AND EVEN FOUR COTTON WHITE MICE!

MISS SHEILA WAS PLEASED WITH HIM...

GOOD, LITTLE SHAMBU. I CAN SEE YOU ARE WORKING VERY HARD. THE PUMPKIN LOOKS QUITE REAL.

THANK YOU, MA'AM.

...BUT LITTLE J.J. WAS NOT.

LITTLE SHAMBU IS GETTING TO BE A REAL HERO. LET ME TEACH HIM A LESSON. AH! A PET SHOP!

LITTLE J.J. BOUGHT FOUR REAL WHITE MICE FROM THE PET SHOP.

EAT, MY LITTLE ONES. GROW BIG AND FAT AND SCARY HEE...HEE...

GOOD BOY!

SQUEAK!

SQUEAK!

FOOD BOY!

THE ANNUAL DAY SOON ARRIVED.

Annual Day

DEAR PARENTS, WE NOW PRESENT - CINDERELLA!

CLAP!

CLAP!

CLAP!

57

THE PLAY BEGAN. BACKSTAGE —

HEY, LITTLE SHAMBU, LOOK AT THIS – FOUR REAL MICE INSTEAD OF THE COTTON ONES. THEY WILL LOOK MORE REAL ON STAGE.

HUH? BUT WHAT WILL MISS SHEILA SAY?

SHE'LL BE HAPPY WITH YOU.

THE PLAY BEGAN. THEN —

BRING ME A PUMPKIN AND FOUR WHITE MICE, CINDERELLA.

YES, FAIRY GODMOTHER.

LITTLE SHAMBU, PUT THE MICE ON TO THE STAGE.

Y... YES, MISS SHEILA.

HE PUT THE BOX OF MICE DOWN.

AS LITTLE SHANTI LIFTED A MOUSE —

HERE YOU ARE, FAIRY GOD...

SQUEAK SQUEAK

EEEKS! A REAL MOUSE!

EEEKS!

AND —

PLOP

58

AAAIEE!

HEELP! RUN RUN!

THERE WAS UTTER CHAOS IN THE AUDITORIUM...

LOOK OUT, A MOUSE IS RUNNING UP YOUR CHAIR.

...TILL FINALLY THE POOR TERRIFIED MICE MANAGED TO FIND A QUIET CORNER.

SQUEAK SQUEAK

MISS SHEILA WAS RED WITH ANGER.

WHO PLAYED THIS SILLY JOKE? WHO BROUGHT THOSE WHITE MICE HERE?

MUST BE LITTLE SHAMBU, MA'AM.

MISS SHEILA, IT WASN'T ME.

BEFORE MISS SHEILA COULD SPEAK ANY FURTHER—

SQUEAK

GOOD BOY!

SQUEAK

FOOD BOY!

ARE THESE MICE YOURS, LITTLE J.J.? YOU ARE A VERY BAD OWNER. THEY COULD HAVE BEEN CRUSHED UNDER OUR FEET. I'M TAKING THEM AWAY.

ER... BUT ... ER...

LATER THAT DAY—

CHILDREN, WE HAVE FOUR NEW MEMBERS IN OUR CLASS. THESE WHITE MICE. THEY WILL BE OUR CLASS PETS.

YIPPEE, I WILL FEED THEM TODAY.

I WILL FEED THEM TOMORROW.

# LITTLE SHAMBU
## DUM DUM TO THE RESCUE

Story and Script:
Reena I. Puri

Illustrations:
Savio Mascarenhas

A LOUD DISCUSSION WAS GOING ON IN LITTLE SHAMBU'S HOUSE.

ISN'T OUR SON ENOUGH? WHY DO YOU WANT TO KEEP CHICKENS?

I WANT TO.

LET'S SEE WHO WINS.

LITTLE SHAMBU'S MOTHER HAD DECIDED THAT SHE WANTED TO EAT FRESH EGGS.

DID YOU KNOW THAT EGG-LAYING HENS ON FARMS ARE KEPT IN TINY CAGES AND NEVER LET OUT?

BUT...

MUM'S GOING STRONG.

NO 'BUTS'. IF I EAT EGGS IT WILL BE FROM FREE AND HAPPY HENS, NOT IMPRISONED AND SAD ONES.

ROUND ONE GOES TO MOM.

ARF!

STOP MUTTERING AND GO AND PLAY.

YES, PA.

IT'LL BE FUN HAVING HENS, DUM DUM. BUT YOU MUST NOT CHASE THEM.

62

# Little Shambu
# CIRCUS RESCUE

**Story and Script: Reena I. Puri**

**Illustrations: Savio Mascarenhas**

LITTLE SHAMBU WAS HAVING A BAD DAY.

DIRTY SOCKS SHOULD BE PUT FOR WASHING. NOT STUFFED UNDER YOUR MATTRESS!

THOSE FOOTPRINTS IN MY FLOWER BED ARE YOURS. DON'T TRY TO TELL ME THAT IT WAS THE YETI.

AFTER SOME TIME—

WHEW! THAT WAS TOUGH, DUM DUM. ALL THAT SCOLDING HAS MADE ME HUNGRY.

SOON —

I'LL STUFF ALL MY POCKETS WITH POPCORN AND THEN WE'LL GO ON AN ADVENTURE TREK.

WOOF! WOOF!

LITTLE SHAMBU DODGED KIDNAPPERS...

...FOUGHT WILD ANIMALS...

...AND ESCAPED ALIEN SPACESHIPS...

WAA... WAA...

64

...TILL HE FINALLY REACHED AN OPEN GROUND.

LOOK AT ALL THOSE TENTS, DUM DUM. MAYBE IT IS THE KING OF ARABIA COME TO PAY US A VISIT.

IT WAS NOT THE KING OF ARABIA. IT WAS A TRAVELLING CIRCUS.

THAT FAT MAN MUST BE THE KING. LET'S SPY ON HIM. HE MAY BE PLANNING A BATTLE.

THE FAT MAN WAS THE OWNER OF THE CIRCUS.

LISTEN TO ME CAREFULLY. THE INSPECTORS ARE COMING TO CHECK US. THE ANIMALS HAVE TO BE MADE INVISIBLE. THEY MUST NOT BE SEEN.

OH! OH! HE IS A MAGICIAN. HE CAN MAKE THINGS INVISIBLE. HIDE, DUM DUM! HE'LL MAKE YOU DISAPPEAR.

YIP!

AFTER A WHILE, A LARGE VAN ARRIVED AND MANY IMPORTANT LOOKING PEOPLE GOT OUT.

HELLO... HELLO... HELLO... HELLO...

HMM!

ALL THE MEN DISAPPEARED INTO A TENT.

NOW WE CAN EXPLORE, DUM DUM. COME ON!

66

67

# THE ALIEN

### The Adventures of Little Shambu

Readers' Choice

Based on a story sent by:
**Anisha Hariharan,**
Mulund (W), Mumbai

Illustrations:
**Savio Mascarenhas**

LITTLE SHAMBU WAS FEELING LOW.

(SIGH!)

THIS IS THE PERFECT WEATHER FOR A COZY SNOOZE...

...BUT... BUT... HERE I AM, DOING MY HOMEWORK, BAHI AND ALL BECAUSE I BROKE MA'S JAPANESE VASE.

...OR A PLATE OF GOLDEN, CRISP, HOT FRENCH FRIES...

WOOF!

...OR A CURL-UP IN FRONT OF MY FAVOURITE TV PROGRAMME...

MAYBE SHE ISN'T SO-O-O ANGRY ANYMORE, DUM DUM. MAYBE WE SHOULD CHECK HER OUT.

WOOF! WOOF!

LITTLE SHAMBU CREPT DOWN THE STAIRS.

THEY ARE WATCHING TELEVISION!

JUST THEN —

R-R-R-UMBLE
BOOM
CRASH

YEOW!

YIP!

EEEP! THE ELECTRICITY IS GONE.

LET'S GET BACK TO OUR ROOM OR WE'LL BE IN DEEP TROUBLE.

BUT —

WHAT IS THAT?

(WHINE)

A STRANGE FIGURE SAT ON A WINDOW.

(CHATTER... CHATTER...) I AM SCARED! MY TEETH ARE CHATTERING.

CHATTER CHATTER

IT IS MAKING SOUNDS LIKE MY CHATTERING TEETH.

THE CONFUSED MONKEY LEAPT OUT THROUGH THE WINDOW.